Fox on a box

Russell Punter
Adapted from a story by Phil Roxbee Cox
Illustrated by Stephen Cartwright

Designed by Helen Cooke
Edited by Jenny Tyler and Lesley Sims
Reading consultants: Alison Kelly and Anne Washtell

There is a little yellow duck to find on every page.

"I need a tasty treat," thinks Fox.

Among the trees, he sees a box.

Fox hops on top.
It helps him reach...

...a sweet and
juicy golden
peach!

Jake's
Bakery

Oh no! Poor Fox slips off instead.

The peach lands, 'SPLAT!'
right on his head.

Now Fox sees eggs inside Hen's nest.

"She won't miss one. I'll leave the rest."

Fox clambers up to nab a snack.

He's almost there, when Hen flies back.

Hen clucks loudly with a frown.
So Fox lets go...

...and tumbles down.

Fox sees a bees' nest in a tree.
"I'll take some honey for my tea."

The nest falls down
and out bees pour.

Poor Fox gets stung.
His skin feels sore.

"I wish that I could catch a fish."

Fox licks his lips. His whiskers twitch.

A fishing rod is quick to make.
Fox puts his box beside the lake.

Hungry Duck tugs on his line.
"Keep off!" she cries.

Fox looks around the streets nearby.

Jake's
Bakery

Then he smells something way up high.

Look! Ted's three steaming pies are fine.
Fox reaches up...

Mmm, this one's mine!

But Pup runs by and hits the box.

"Watch out, you'll knock me off!" shouts Fox.

Fox lands, head first, inside the box.

"A fruit cake broke my fall. I'm fine.

My treat was with me all the time!"

Puzzles

Puzzle 1

What does Fox want in each picture?

1.
2.

3.
4.

a peach
honey
a pie
an egg

Puzzle 2

Which box contained the cake?

1. Jane's Bakery
2. Jake's Bakery
3. James's Bakery

Puzzle 3
Where is Fox?

1.

2.

3.

| on the box | beside the box | in the box |

Puzzle 4
Which five things are <u>not</u> in the picture?

Fox   pie
peach   Hen
wall   bee
nest   eggs
honey   Pup

Answers to puzzles

Puzzle 1

1.

a pie

2.

an egg

3.

honey

4.

a peach

Puzzle 2

Box number 2 contained the cake.

Jake's Bakery

Puzzle 3

1.

beside the box

2.

in the box

3.

on the box

Puzzle 4
These five things are <u>not</u> in the picture:

peach

honey

pie

bee

Pup

About phonics

Phonics is a method of teaching reading used extensively in today's schools. At its heart is an emphasis on identifying the *sounds* of letters, or combinations of letters, that are then put together to make words. These sounds are known as phonemes.

Starting to read

Learning to read is an important milestone for any child. The process can begin well before children start to learn letters and put them together to read words. The sooner children can discover books and enjoy stories and language, the better they will be prepared for reading themselves, first with the help of an adult and then independently.

You can find out more about phonics on the Usborne Very First Reading website, **usborne.com/veryfirstreading** (US readers go to **veryfirstreading.com**). Click on the **Parents** tab at the top of the page, then scroll down and click on **About synthetic phonics**.

Phonemic awareness

An important early stage in pre-reading and early reading is developing phonemic awareness: that is, listening out for the sounds within words. Rhymes, rhyming stories and alliteration are excellent ways of encouraging phonemic awareness.

In this story, your child will soon identify the *o* sound, as in **fox** and **box**. Look out, too, for rhymes such as **reach** – **peach** and **wish** – **fish**.

Hearing your child read

If your child is reading a story to you, don't rush to correct mistakes, but be ready to prompt or guide if he or she is struggling. Above all, give plenty of praise and encouragement.